Now I'm Big!

Now I'

m Big!

karen katz

Margaret K. McElderry Books

New York   London   Toronto   Sydney   New Delhi

MARGARET K. McELDERRY BOOKS
An imprint of Simon & Schuster Children's Publishing Division
1230 Avenue of the Americas, New York, New York 10020
Copyright © 2013 by Karen Katz
MARGARET K. McELDERRY BOOKS is a trademark of Simon & Schuster, Inc.
For information about special discounts for bulk purchases, please contact
Simon & Schuster Special Sales at 1-866-506-1949 or
business@simonandschuster.com.
The Simon & Schuster Speakers Bureau can bring authors to your live event.
For more information or to book an event, contact the Simon & Schuster
Speakers Bureau at 1-866-248-3049 or visit our website at
www.simonspeakers.com.
Book design by Ann Bobco
The text for this book is set in Ad Lib BT.
The illustrations for this book are rendered in watercolor and gouache.
Manufactured in China
1212 SCP
2 4 6 8 10 9 7 5 3 1
Library of Congress Cataloging-in-Publication Data
Katz, Karen.
Now I'm big! / Karen Katz.—1st ed.
p. cm.
Summary: A little girl contrasts all of the amazing things she can do for
herself that had to be done for her when she was a baby,
from dressing herself to reading to her baby sister.
ISBN 978-1-4169-3547-6 (hardcover)
ISBN 978-1-4424-7165-8 (eBook)
[1. Growth—Fiction. 2. Babies—Fiction] I. Title. II. Title: Now I am big.
PZ7.K15745Np 2013
[E]—dc23
2011047256

FIRST
EDITION

To my Lena bean . . .

all grown up and wonderful.

I used to be a baby.

When I was a baby Daddy put on my booties and snapped my snaps.

NOW I'M BIG!
I can snap my snaps
and zip my zippers all by myself.

When
I was a baby
I drank
from a bottle

and ate
with my fingers.

What
a
mess!

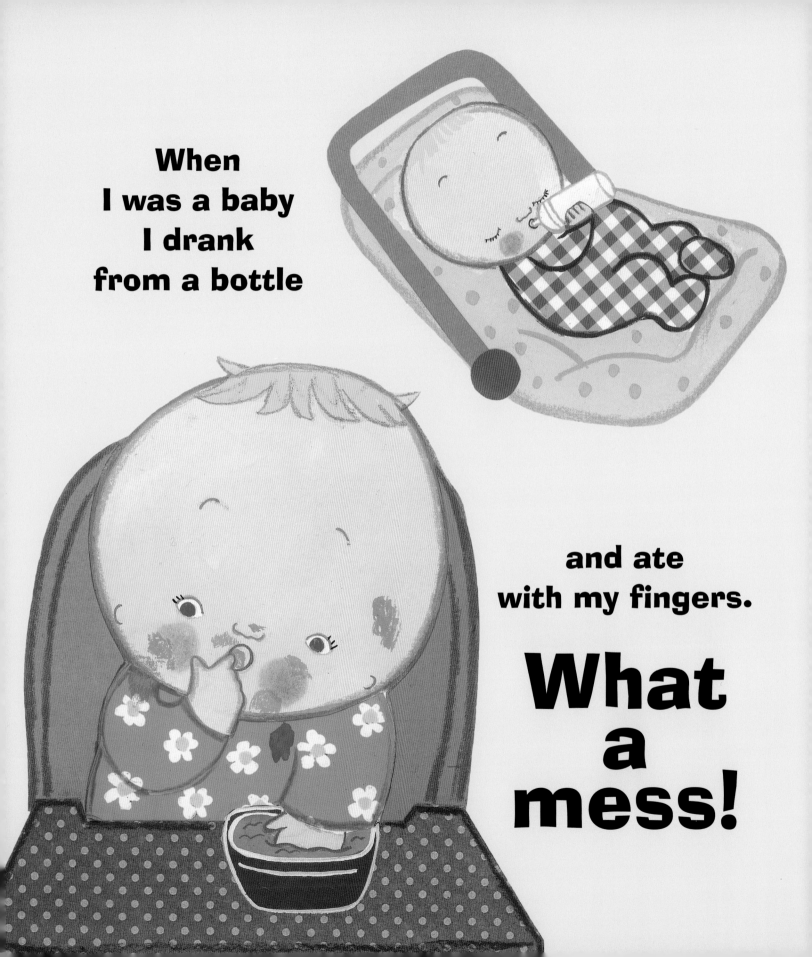

NOW I'M BIG!
I can eat with a fork and a spoon,
and drink from a cup!

When
I was a baby
I had to
wear diapers.

NOW I'M BIG!

I can wear real underpants and poo in the toilet.

When
I was a baby
I could
only crawl,

and all I could say
was *Da-da*
and *Ma-ma.*

NOW I'M BIG!

I can run

and jump

and spin

and talk!

When I was a baby I chewed on

EVERYTHING—

books,
toys,
and grass.

NOW I'M BIG!

I can read my books,

play
with my
toys,

and
roll in the
grass.

**When I was a baby I played
by myself in a playpen.**

NOW I'M BIG!

I can play with lots of friends in the park.

When I was a baby
Mommy pushed me
in a stroller.

NOW
I'M BIG!

I can ride
my own bike . . .

and
I walk
with
Mommy,
but
I ALWAYS
hold
her hand.

When
I was a baby
Mommy had to
wash me.

NOW I'M BIG!

I can wash myself

and
dry off
with my favorite
towel.

When I was a baby
I slept in a tiny baby's crib.

NOW I'M BIG!

I sleep by myself
in my own
BIG BED
and . . .

NOW
I have
a new
baby
sister!

I can
help her
put on her
booties,

**snap
her snaps,**

**and
wash her face.**

**I can
help her drink
from
her bottle**

and I can read her stories.

There's
so much I can do...

now
that
I'm
BIG!